To Ma and Baba...and the sempiternal child in all of us.
Tutu

With love for Arturo.
Martina

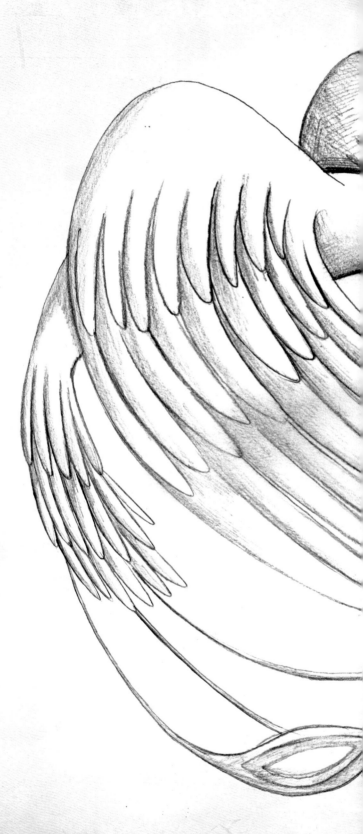

First published in the United Kingdom in 2015 by
Lantana Publishing Ltd., London.

Text © Tutu Dutta 2015
Illustration © Martina Peluso 2015

ISBN: 978-0-9932253-4-5

A CIP catalogue record for this book is available from the British Library.
Printed in Hong Kong.

This book can be ordered directly from the publishers from the website:
www.lantanapublishing.com

Tutu Dutta & **Martina Peluso**

PHOENIX
song

LANTANA
PUBLISHING

Arohan walked home from his flute lesson with his cousin, Mei Mei. He sighed and wished his parents would buy him a guitar for his birthday.

At that moment, the wind carried the sound of rustling bamboo leaves from the hill behind their home.

Mei Mei shivered. "Grandma said that the hill is protected by a guardian spirit. Anyone who disturbs the forest will be swallowed up by the trees! You have to be very respectful when you enter the bamboo grove..."

"Happy birthday, Arohan!"

Arohan unwrapped his presents, one by one.
The last present from Grandma caught
his eye. Underneath the wrapping was a
wooden box.

"You have the gift, Arohan," Grandma
said softly. "Make sure you play with
your heart."

Arohan took out the flute. He stared at
it for a few seconds, the tears welling up
behind his eyes. Then he dropped it back in
its box and ran to his room.

"Arohan? Why did you run out like that?" asked his mother.

"Ma, I just don't want to play the flute anymore! I want a guitar!"

"*Sayang*, you know we can't afford a guitar," said his mother gently. "Besides, Miss Wong thinks you're very talented. It would be a waste to give up now."

Arohan groaned.

His mother tried again. "It's a special flute – a family heirloom from Grandma. It's called a *xiao*."

Arohan looked at the flute. "But it looks like an ordinary bamboo flute to me."

"Ah, the *xiao* is no ordinary flute…"

"There is a legend about the *xiao*. Long ago in China, there was a man who roamed the forests with the birds and wild animals. He had a very special gift. Whenever he played the *xiao*, he could summon the phoenix."

Arohan sat up. "The phoenix? That's a kind of magical bird, right?"

"Yes. The phoenix represents spring and the renewal of life. Here it is known as Cendrawasih. It is said that even dead trees come to life when it sings," she added.

"Ma, I'm eight now. Too old for fairy tales," Arohan replied.

His mother smiled, and told him to rejoin the party.

"Still wish it was a guitar," Arohan grumbled to himself.

A few weeks later, Arohan's mother and father left for Kuala Lumpur for the weekend. Arohan's older brothers were feeling bored.

"We have the entire day to ourselves with nothing to do..." said Rajuna.

Shan grinned. "I know! Let's climb the hill!"

Arohan overheard his brothers' plans and decided to follow them.

"The bamboo is whispering something!" said Shan in a low voice. "I've heard that the bamboo grove is haunted by a guardian spirit..."

Rajuna laughed. "Don't tell me you're scared of a silly old superstition? Come on, let's race!"

Oh no! thought Arohan. *They're disturbing the forest!*

Arohan was too afraid to enter the forest. The bamboo leaves were rustling fiercely. Remembering what Mei Mei had told him, he pressed his palms together and bowed.

"O Guardian of the Forest, please allow me to enter. I promise not to harm any living thing!"

He looked around but his brothers were nowhere to be seen.

Where did they go? he wondered.

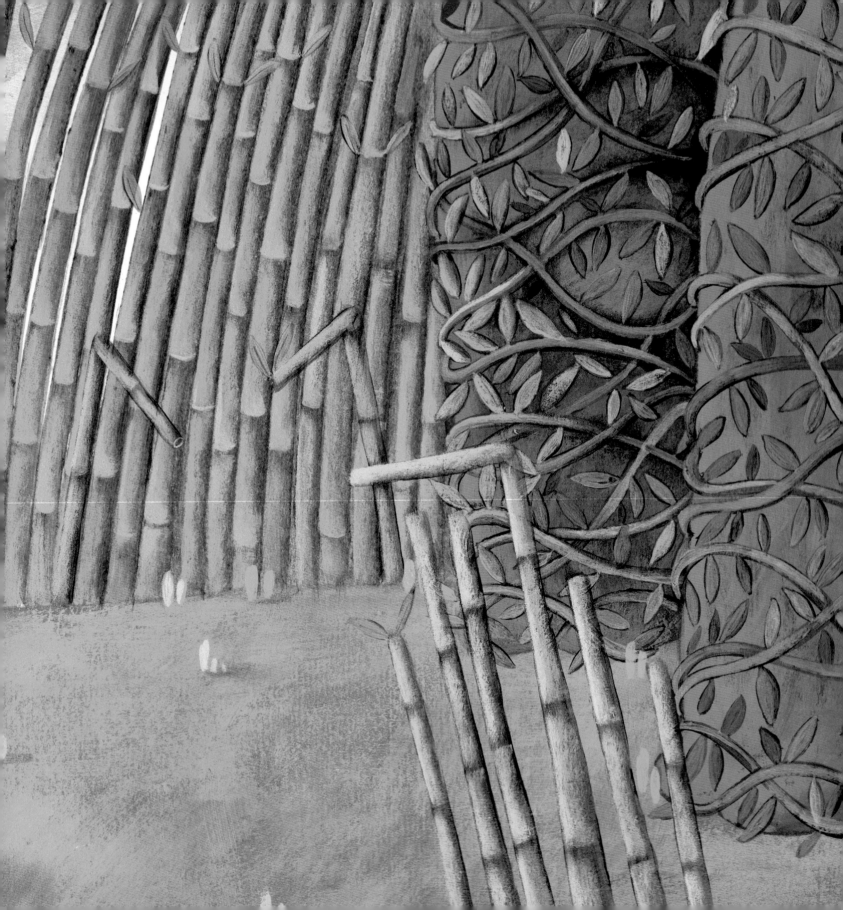

"Rajuna? Shan?" Arohan couldn't believe his eyes. "What's happened to you?"

It was just as Mei Mei had said. His brothers had disturbed the forest and been swallowed up by the trees!

Arohan remembered his mother's story about Cendrawasih. If the phoenix could bring dead trees back to life, could it help his brothers?

"But that was just a fairy tale!" he said out loud. "Wasn't it?"

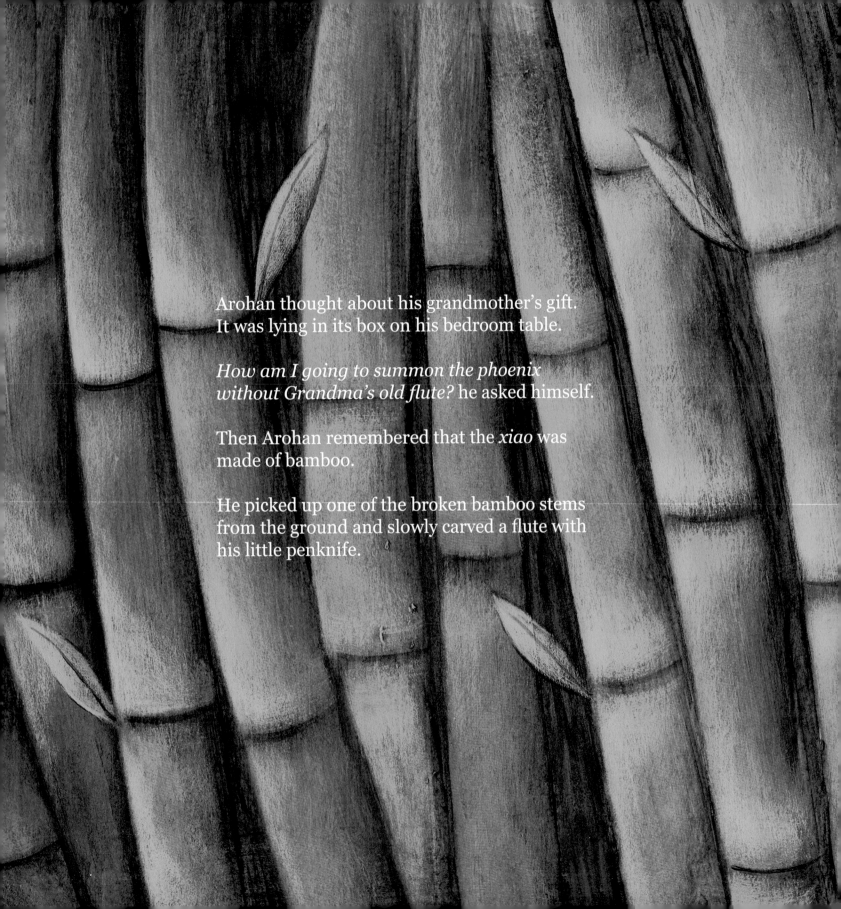

Arohan thought about his grandmother's gift.
It was lying in its box on his bedroom table.

*How am I going to summon the phoenix
without Grandma's old flute?* he asked himself.

Then Arohan remembered that the *xiao* was
made of bamboo.

He picked up one of the broken bamboo stems
from the ground and slowly carved a flute with
his little penknife.

Arohan played an old song Miss Wong had taught him.
But nothing happened.

"It's not working!" he said, with tears in his eyes. "I can't do it!"

And then he thought of his grandmother's words on his birthday.
"Grandma believes I have the gift," he whispered to himself.

Arohan wiped away his tears and put all his heart into his music.

He played the flute as he had never played it before and the entire forest echoed with his music...

Arohan stopped playing the flute because a more wonderful song had enveloped the hill.

"Cendrawasih!" he sighed.

The vines that had covered Rajuna and Shan slowly fell away,
releasing the two boys. They opened their eyes.

"Rajuna! Shan!" Arohan cried out,
running towards his brothers.

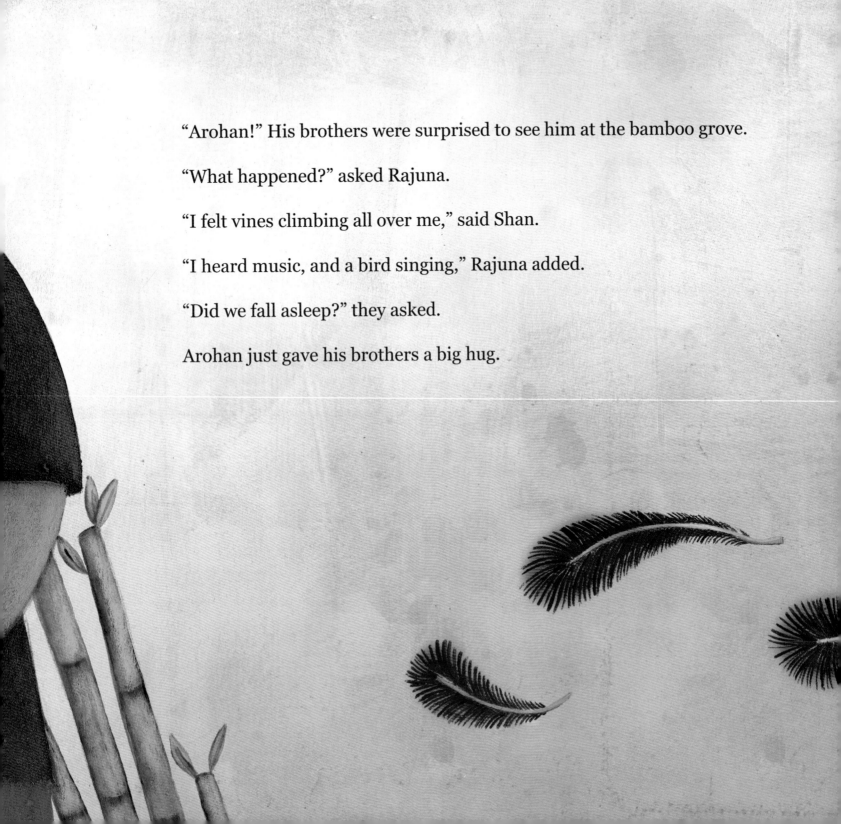

"Arohan!" His brothers were surprised to see him at the bamboo grove.

"What happened?" asked Rajuna.

"I felt vines climbing all over me," said Shan.

"I heard music, and a bird singing," Rajuna added.

"Did we fall asleep?" they asked.

Arohan just gave his brothers a big hug.

As they walked back down the hill, Rajuna took the flute from Arohan.

"Did you make this yourself?" he asked. "I thought you hated the flute!"

"Actually," replied Arohan with a smile, "I think I might just give it another chance."